LITTLE ARTIST
GRUMPY PETS

This book belongs to

_____

Scan the QR Code below or go to www.begoodbooks.com
for FREE WORKSHEETS

COLORING BOOK

LITTLE ARTIST

GRUMPY PETS

This book belongs to

COLORING BOOK

BE GOOD BOOKS
BeGoodBooks.com

Don't Even Think About it

Made in the USA
Monee, IL
27 December 2024

75495266R00063